BLUE BUG'S BEACH PARTY

by Virginia Poulet

illustrated by Stan Fleming & Mary Maloney

 CHILDRENS PRESS, CHICAGO

For Didier, Chris and Cathy

Library of Congress Cataloging in Publication Data

Poulet, Virginia.
  Blue Bug's beach party.

  SUMMARY: Before they can have their beach party,
Blue Bug and his friends have to clean the litter off
the beach.
  [1. Litter (Trash)—Fiction] I. Fleming, Stanley,
ill. II. Maloney, Mary P., ill. III. Title.
PZ7.P86BI   [E]   74-31224
ISBN 0-516-03423-5

13 14 15 16 17 18 19 20 R 99 98 97 96 95 94 93 92

BLUE BUG'S
BEACH PARTY

4

Blue Bug and his friends

had to pull,

move,

9

drag,

carry,

tug,

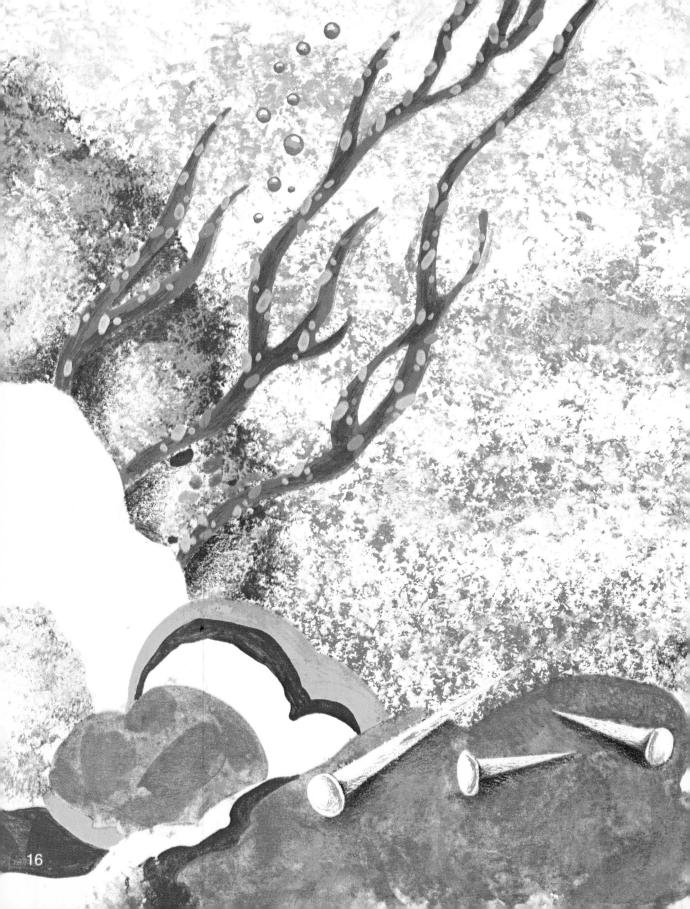

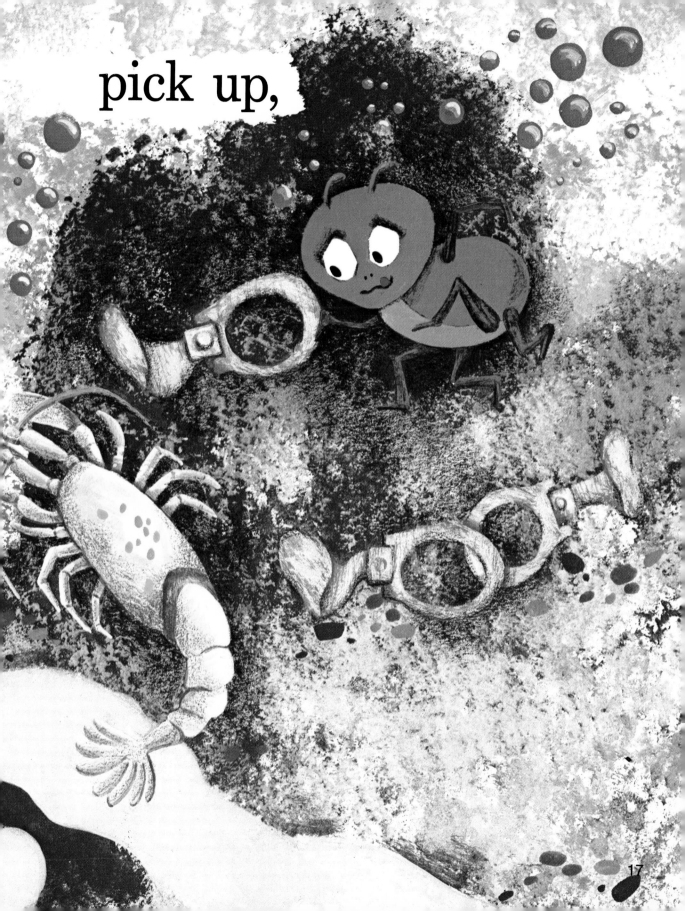

pick up,

17

load,

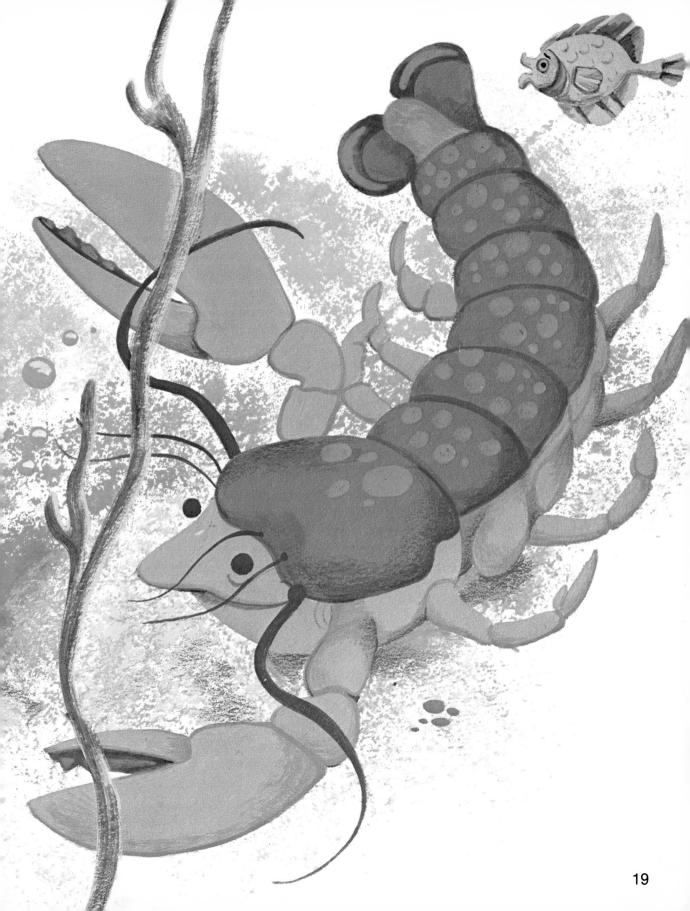

push,

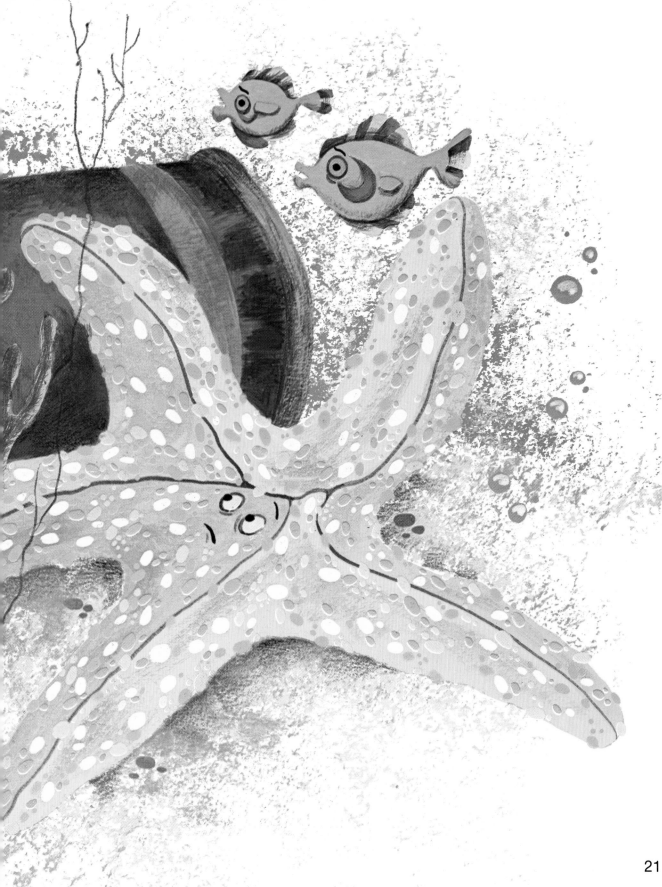

huff and puff,

23

and work hard

24

to clean the beach
for their party !

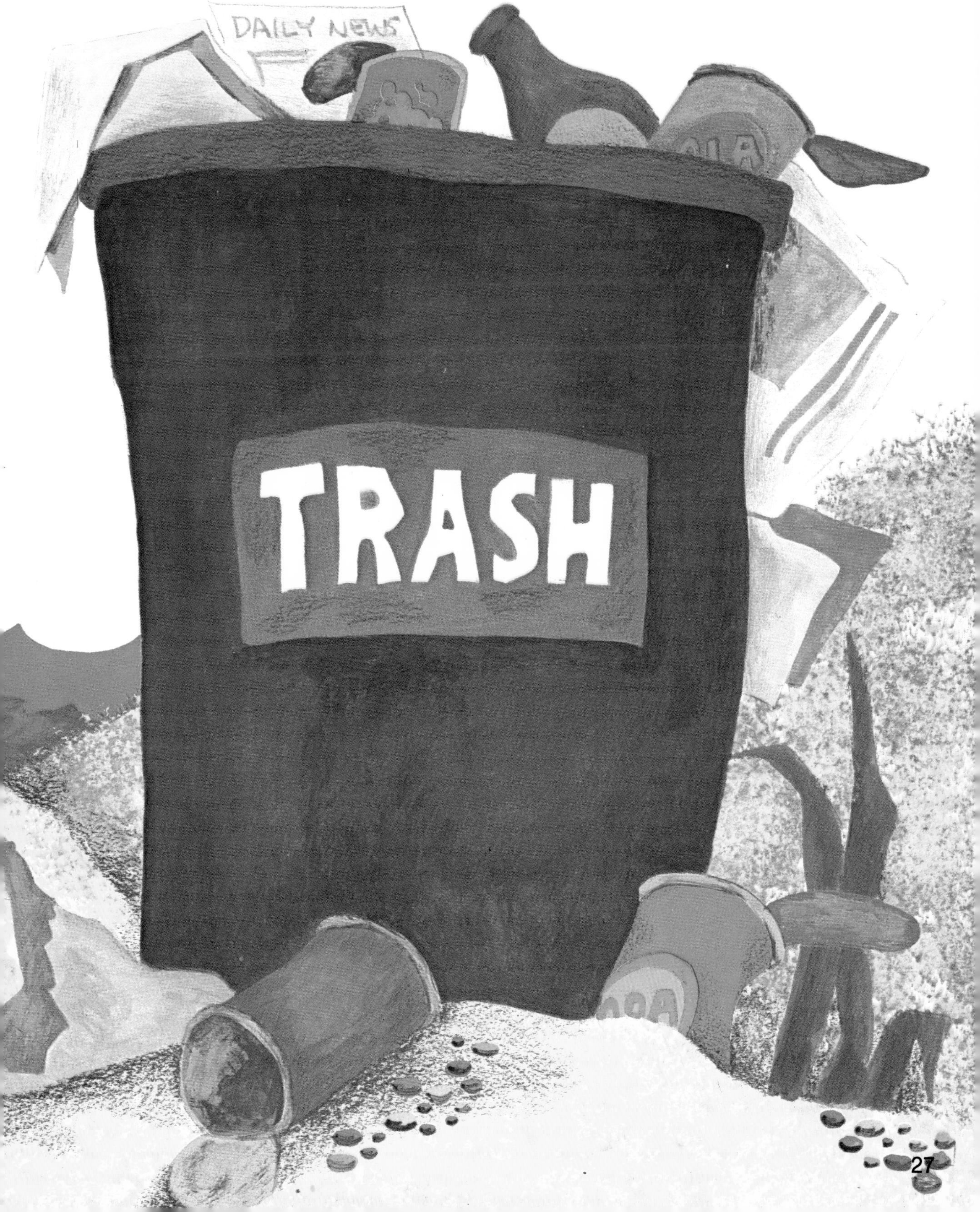
DAILY NEWS
TRASH

Will you help keep

their home clean?

Be a Blue Bug Helper

sandpiper

hermit crab

clam

seagull

shrimp

lobster

crab

starfish

mud snail

sandhopper

plover

31

About the Author:

Virginia Poulet lives in Tulsa, Oklahoma, with her husband and two young children. After graduating as a fashion design major from Washington University in St. Louis, she designed women's lingerie for a year, then worked in Morocco for two years with the Peace Corps. Having observed that a child just beginning to read is often overwhelmed and intimidated by a mass of words on a page, Ms. Poulet wanted to provide simple yet stimulating beginning readers that would give a child a feeling of accomplishment and give him courage to go on to something harder. She developed the four Blue Bug books so that the child might put his newly acquired reading skills to use as soon as possible; to let the beginning reader reassure himself that he can, indeed, master a real book.

About the Artists:

Mary Maloney was born in Chicago, and she received her Bachelor of Fine Arts from Northern Illinois University in 1970. A year of travel followed which included Europe, North Africa, Iceland and Israel. Mary took a great many photographs during that year, particularly of young people. She came to believe that "the essence of a country can be found in the faces of its children" through their openness and curiosity. She now lives in San Francisco, and hopes to continue photographing and illustrating for children.

Stan Fleming was born in Medicine Hat, Alberta, Canada. After his high school graduation in Canada he secured a scholarship at the school of Fine Arts at the University of Alberta. He also graduated from the Art Institute of Chicago. He opened his own art and photography studio in Chicago in 1952 and since then his work has appeared in innumerable books and magazines.